Lizzie McGuire
THE 'RENTS

Adapted by Alice Alfonsi

Based on the television series, "Lizzie McGuire", created by Terri Minsky

Part One is based on the episode written by Douglas Tuber & Tim Maile

Part Two is based on the epiosde written by Melissa Gould

Watch it on
DISNEY CHANNEL
abc Kids

DISNEY PRESS

VOLO

New York

Printed in the United States of America

First Edition
1 3 5 7 9 10 8 6 4 2

Library of Congress Catalog Card Number on file.

ISBN 0-7868-4681-X
For more Disney Press fun, visit www.disneybooks.com
Visit DisneyChannel.com

PART ONE

CHAPTER ONE

"Listen to me! All of you!" cried Mr. Dig.

Lizzie McGuire and her half-asleep classmates jerked fully upright at their desks. Whoa, what is *up* with Mr. Dig? thought Lizzie. Too much coffee at lunch?

Mr. Dig, Lizzie's substitute teacher, paced the classroom, then stopped and threw his hands into the air. "Turn off your TVs! Read a book!" he shouted.

Lizzie glanced uneasily at her two best

friends. David "Gordo" Gordon didn't seem fazed by Mr. Dig's directive. Miranda Sanchez, however, seemed annoyed. She pursed her lips and raised her hand. "Hey," she stated defensively, "I just read something last week."

"Miss Sanchez," snapped Mr. Dig, "the latest issue of some new fanzine doesn't count."

Miranda winced and shrank down in her seat.

Whoa, Lizzie thought, Mr. Dig's really got the 411 on this class.

"What about *you*, Mr. Gordon?" the teacher challenged, pointing an accusatory finger at Gordo. "What have *you* read in the last week?"

"*One Hundred Years of Solitude, On the Road, Seven Pillars of Wisdom*, and *Schnozzola: The Jimmy Durante Story*," Gordo instantly rattled off.

Mr. Dig blinked, surprised, at Gordo. "I was trying to make the point that you kids don't read enough," he said. "You kind of cut my legs off there."

"Oh," said Gordo with a shrug. "Sorry about that."

Note to Mr. Dig, thought Lizzie, here are a few things on which you *never* want to challenge Gordo: being well-read, completing required homework, and movie trivia.

"I'm assigning a book report," Mr. Dig stated flatly.

The class groaned.

Why are they groaning? I like reading. . . . *Harry Potter*, *Eloise*, books about cats that solve crimes—it's schoolwork you can do lying down.

"I want all the girls to read *The Orchids and Gumbo Poker Club*," Mr. Dig declared, "which is about mother-daughter relationships and social climbing."

Now it was Lizzie's turn to groan. "Mother-daughter relationships?" she muttered, rolling her eyes.

This is starting to sound like one of those open-and-shut books. I'm going to want to shut it as soon as I open it!

"And I want all the boys to read *A River Runs Through It*," Mr. Dig continued, "which is about father-son relationships. And trout."

Gordo nodded happily. He liked trout. "That's g-o-o-d eatin'," he joked.

Lizzie leaned toward Miranda. "I actually

like reading," she whispered, "but about mother-daughter relationships? I get enough of that at home."

As far as Lizzie was concerned, her relationship with her mother mostly came down to a few simple daily phrases: brush your teeth, clean your room, get good grades, clear the table, and the answer "no" to anything that costs money.

Later that evening, Lizzie went to her room and settled on her bed with *The Orchids and Gumbo Poker Club*. She opened the cover with a heavy sigh, not wanting to read one line, let alone seven whole chapters. But Mr. Dig was going to grade her on a book report, so she forced herself to forge ahead.

Chapter One, Lizzie read silently to herself. *Defining moments. They come and go in our lives like streetcars and summer breezes. Like the sweet, subtle blush on a honeysuckle blossom—here for the most fleeting of instants . . . then gone again. Do we pick these moments? Or do they pick us?*

Lizzie sat up a little straighter. This is actually sort of interesting, she thought. I mean, I can relate because I'm always thinking about how certain crucial moments will define my own life. It's like, what will be the ultimate consequence of my not making the cheerleading squad? Or deciding to quit rhythmic gymnastics? Or tripping over a garbage can in front of Ethan Craft?

Lizzie continued reading *Orchids*, and by the end of chapter one, she was completely hooked. The story was about a young woman named Darcy Lou, who lived on the Louisiana bayou with her mother, Tallulah. Darcy Lou and her mother were poor, but they were very close, so when Darcy fell in love with a wealthy boy from a prominent New Orleans family, her mother vowed to do everything in her power to make Darcy's dream come true.

"*Darcy Lou quietly removed her gloves, set them on the divan, and blew out the candle*," Lizzie whispered after a solid hour of reading. "*After that, there was only night, and stars, and the memory of love.*" End of chapter five.

Lizzie swallowed. She hadn't expected the book to be such a tearjerker. Mr. Dig should have warned us to have a box of tissues nearby, she thought before bursting into waves of sentimental weeping.

"It's so beautiful!" Lizzie cried. "She's so sad! She loves her mom!"

That's so beautiful!

CHAPTER TWO

While Lizzie spent the rest of her evening totally engrossed in Darcy Lou's story, Lizzie's little brother spent it being totally bored.

"We're in a lull, Lanny," said Matt McGuire, sitting on his bed. "We need to come up with something to do."

For the past hour, Matt and his best friend, Lanny, had been trying to toss playing cards into a wastebasket. They were also trying to dream up their next big project. Not only had they come up with nothing, but every single card they'd thrown had missed the basket.

Lanny, who never seemed to speak, sighed and pursed his lips. Matt, who could read his silent friend's thoughts better than a carnival clairvoyant, nodded knowingly and said, "You're right. It's the wrong time of the year for rocket-powered skiing."

For another few minutes, they sat in silence. Then Matt threw up his hands. "C'mon, there's got to be *something* we can do. Think . . . think, think, think. . . ."

As the boys sat thinking, a two-foot-high chimpanzee wearing a pair of khaki shorts and a green T-shirt appeared at the open window. The little chimp climbed across the ledge, scrambled onto Matt's bed, and plopped down as if he owned the place.

Matt and Lanny looked down at the chimp now sitting between them. The chimp curled its lips and sneered. Matt cocked an eyebrow. "Now we've got a chimp," he told Lanny. "*That's* something to work with."

Lanny nodded.

Matt didn't know where the chimp had come from, but at the moment he didn't care. It was the beginning of the end of boredom. "This is so cool!" he cried. But first things first, he told himself. Time for introductions. "Hiya, little fellow, my name's Matt, and this is Lanny—"

Matt held out his hand, but the rude little animal didn't shake. Instead, he stuck out his tongue and blew air through his lips, giving Matt and Lanny a raspberry.

"Hey, don't do that," scolded Matt. "We're just trying to be friends."

The chimp screeched, waved his arms, and began to run around the room, knocking things over.

"Hey! No! Cool it," called Matt. "What did we do?"

But the chimp ignored Matt. He pulled down Matt's indoor basketball net, scattered craft supplies, bowled over action figures, and finally picked up a ceramic lamp and dropped it on the floor. *Crash!* The lamp broke into a dozen pieces.

Matt was horrified by the mess the animal had made—and even more horrified when he heard his father stomping up the stairs.

Matt's bedroom door swung open, and Mr. McGuire stood there looking like a bubbling volcano. Matt and Lanny sat frozen, waiting for the eruption.

"All right," Mr. McGuire said sharply. "How many times do I have to tell you guys to keep it down?" Earlier, the boys had been playing a CD too loudly, which had prompted Mr. McGuire's first trip up the stairs—and he was not at all happy about making a second.

"Who did that?" he asked, pointing to a broken lamp.

Matt jerked his thumb behind him and said, "He did."

"Who?" asked Mr. McGuire.

"The chimp," said Matt, but when he turned his head, he realized the raspberry-blowing beastie had already bounced off the mattress and out the window. "There was a monkey in here," Matt quickly told his father. "And he ran around, went nuts, and busted my lamp."

Mr. McGuire's eyes flared angrily behind his wire-rimmed glasses.

"You going to stick with that story?" Sam McGuire asked. "'Cause if you are, the lamp's coming out of your allowance."

Matt's jaw dropped. His father didn't

believe him, he realized. But this mess wasn't his fault!

"Now, quit roughhousing," Mr. McGuire warned.

"B-but—" Matt sputtered.

Slam! Mr. McGuire obviously wasn't interested in any more excuses. He'd simply walked out the door and shut it—*loudly*.

With a frustrated sigh, Matt turned on the bed to look out the window behind him. The chimp's head suddenly popped up. Matt frowned at the animal, who responded by pointing a hairy finger at Matt and laughing.

"Lanny," said Matt, his eyes narrowing. "I think we've got ourselves a *bad* chimpanzee."

Meanwhile, next door, in Lizzie's bedroom, the tearjerker marathon was still going on. The room had grown darker, the shadows longer, but Lizzie barely noticed. The lamp by her bed shone enough light on the pages of *The Orchids and Gumbo Poker Club* for her to continue reading—and that's exactly what she did. . . .

"*Tallulah was on the veranda, with a look on her face like a bayou cloudburst,*" Lizzie whispered. "*Darcy Lou watched her through the French doors, like staring into a thousand futures.*"

At this point in the story, Darcy Lou was preparing to leave her mother and sail away with her new husband to a faraway place. Lizzie could almost smell the cloying scent of the orchids in Tallulah's garden.

Biting her lip, Lizzie finally turned to the book's last page. . . .

"*Momma? I'm fixin' to go now, Momma,*" said Darcy Lou.

"*Before you go, Darcy Lou,*" said Tallulah. "*I*

. . . I . . . I want you to have this. . . ." Tallulah handed Darcy Lou a small box.

Darcy remembered this box. She'd seen it once before—when Tallulah had revealed to Darcy Lou who her father really was.

"Oh, Momma," said Darcy Lou, as she opened the box to look inside. "It's the bracelet Ben Turpin gave you!" Darcy couldn't believe it. She knew how much this bracelet meant to her mother. "Why are you giving it to me, Momma?"

"Oh, sugar," said Tallulah, "wherever you go, well, that's where my heart and soul have to be. And when I die and sink beneath the bayou mud, part of me will always be with you."

With tears in her eyes, Darcy Lou ran to Tallulah and threw herself into her mother's arms. "Oh, Momma, Momma. I want us to be friends! Friends forever."

"Oh, I'm so glad, sweet potato," said Tallulah.

"And I can finally say it—welcome to the Orchids and Gumbo Poker Club."

"Oh, Momma. Oh, it's good to be here, Momma. It is so good to be here," said Darcy Lou, then she kissed her mother one last time.

Someday, Darcy Lou would return to her beloved home. Until then, she knew she'd just have to carry its memory, along with the deep love for her dear mother, safely in her heart. And that's just what she did as she headed right through the front door and into that bright new horizon called the future.

Lizzie shut the book with tear-filled eyes. I feel the very same way as Darcy Lou, she thought. I love my mom *so* much, and I'll be *so* sad if I get married like Darcy Lou and have to move far away and leave her behind. . . . Omigosh, I totally can't stop crying!

I want *my* mom to call me sweet potato and

give me a bracelet filled with special meaning. And I want us to be friends forever, too, Lizzie decided, wiping her eyes.

I know, she told herself at last. My mom and I can start our very own Orchids and Gumbo Poker Club. And I'm totally going to ask her right now. Here I come, "Tallulah"!

CHAPTER THREE

Lizzie flew down the stairs and into the living room, where her parents were watching TV. "Mom! Mom! Mom! Mom!" she cried. "I want to be friends!"

"That's great, sweetie," said Jo McGuire. She turned to her husband on the couch. "Sam, did you hear that?"

"Uh-huh," said Lizzie's father, but his gaze didn't budge from the television screen. "Could she keep it down?" He pointed at the

TV. Mr. McGuire was totally engrossed in the show he was watching. "Whoa," he said, his eyes glued to the set, "would you look at *her*? She is *gorgeous*!"

Mrs. McGuire smiled at Lizzie. "We *are* friends, aren't we, honey?"

"I don't mean 'friends' like you drop me off at soccer practice and I get you a vanilla-scented candle for Mother's Day." Lizzie held up her copy of *Orchids and Gumbo*. "I mean 'friends' like two women that share everything with each other. Like the type of friends that you see on *Oprah*. And we've got to do it *now*, before you sink beneath the bayou mud!"

"How could she *not* make the finals?" Lizzie's father exclaimed, still fixed on the TV. "C'mon, judges! Look at her posture, her poise! She's spectacular!"

Ignoring her husband, Mrs. McGuire tried to answer her daughter as best she could.

"Well, honey, I'm not planning on sinking beneath any mud anytime soon, but if you want to be closer than we already are . . . I can't think of anything I'd rather do."

"Oh!" cried Lizzie, totally psyched. "We'll start our own Orchids and Gumbo Poker Club!"

"Okay," said Mrs. McGuire, slightly bewildered, but game anyway. "Whatever that is, sounds good to me."

"Those stupid judges!" complained Lizzie's father. "How could that German shepherd win Best in Show! The Bernese mountain dog was ten times prettier! That's it! I'm never watching the Westchester Kennel Club again!"

The next morning, Lizzie and her mom kicked off their Orchids and Gumbo Club by going out for a pancake breakfast, then heading to the mall for a day of shopping.

With his wife and daughter gone, Mr. McGuire decided to spend some quality time with his collection of ceramic lawn gnomes. First he touched up the fading paint on their little red cheeks, brightly colored clothing, and tiny garden tools. Then he rearranged their little "gnomes at work" scenes in the front yard.

By noon, Mr. McGuire was very hot and extremely thirsty. He walked into the kitchen for a glass of lemonade—and stopped dead. From the looks of the place, some sort of cyclone had passed through. Chairs were overturned, dishes broken, food scattered, and the garbage can emptied onto the floor.

Mr. McGuire exploded. "Matt! MA-A-A-T-T!"

From the backyard, Matt and Lanny hurried in. "Whoa, what a mess. What happened in here?" said Matt, eyeing the damage.

"Why don't *you* tell me?" barked Mr. McGuire.

Matt took a step backward. My dad's acting like *I* made this mess, he thought. But me and Lanny have been hanging in the backyard for most of the morning.

"*I* didn't do this," Matt told his father.

Mr. McGuire crossed his arms. "Who do you suppose did?"

Matt glanced at Lanny. They shared a knowing look. "You're right, Lanny," said Matt. "It was that dang dirty ape."

Mr. McGuire lost it. "Are you *still* pretending there's some chimpanzee around here doing all the things you don't want to get blamed for?" he yelled.

"But there is," argued Matt.

"That's it," said Mr. McGuire, throwing up his hands. "You're both grounded."

"What!" Matt couldn't believe his dad was

going to punish him for something he didn't do—not to mention his totally innocent best friend. "You can't ground Lanny," Matt pointed out. "He's not your kid."

"You're right," said Mr. McGuire. "*You're* grounded twice as long, Matt. Lanny, help him clean up the kitchen."

"What?" cried Matt.

But Mr. McGuire had already stormed off, leaving the boys alone with the mess. With a sigh of frustration, Matt turned to Lanny. "This is an *evil* chimp," he declared.

Just then, the boys heard a sound coming from a kitchen cupboard. The two rushed over and opened its doors.

There he was, in all his hairy glory. The tiny fiend sprang from the cupboard, making Matt and Lanny jump back. Then the nasty little beast raced across the kitchen. He paused only once, to mock them with a taunting cackle, before disappearing around the corner.

Matt's eyes narrowed. Then, in a deadly serious voice, he told Lanny, "We've got a chimp to catch."

CHAPTER FOUR

Across town, Gordo and Miranda were just sitting down at a table inside the Digital Bean, the cybercafé that was also their favorite hangout. Gordo had bought a basket of french fries, and Miranda had purchased a soda.

"I'm hungry," Miranda realized, smelling Gordo's fries. She reached over and popped some into her mouth.

"Yeah, well, I'm thirsty," said Gordo, and

he drank some of Miranda's soda. She play-
fully shoved his shoulder, then grabbed a few
more of his fries.

"Hey, you guys," called Lizzie. She strode
up to their table and dropped into an empty
chair.

Miranda brightened, ready to greet her best
friend, until she noticed something weird.
Lizzie wasn't alone. "Lizzie's mom is with
her," Miranda whispered to Gordo.

"Hey, Mrs. McGuire," said Gordo, as
Lizzie's mother settled into the last empty
chair at their table.

"She's sitting down!" rasped Miranda in
Gordo's ear.

"Hey, you guys, what's going on?" said
Lizzie's mother with a clueless smile.

"Nothing. Nothing at all," said Gordo
defensively. "We haven't done *anything*."

Omigosh, thought Miranda in a panic. I

know why she's here. She's figured out what happened last week when we were throwing that Nerf football around the McGuires' living room!

"We didn't break your hobo figurine," Miranda blurted out, instantly cracking under pressure.

Gordo gave Miranda a dirty look for coming clean. "It was like that when we got there," he lied.

"It's okay," said Mrs. McGuire. "I never liked it anyway." She shrugged. "Sam's cousin Ree-Ree gave it to me for my birthday."

Gordo was relieved to hear they weren't in trouble, but that still left him seriously confused. If Lizzie's mother isn't here to bust us, he thought, then why *is* she here? "So, uh, Mrs. McGuire, you're dropping Lizzie off?" he fished.

"No, no," said Lizzie, "she's going to hang out with us."

"Why?" Miranda bluntly asked.

"Because we're friends," replied Lizzie. "We hang."

Miranda's mouth gaped in bewildered horror.

"You know what? I'm going to go to the ladies' room and check my makeup," said Mrs. McGuire. Then she turned to Lizzie. "You want to come, sweet potato?"

Lizzie smiled. "I'll be there in a minute, Tallulah," she teased.

After Mrs. McGuire was out of earshot, Gordo turned to Lizzie. "All right, she left. What's *really* going on?" he asked.

"I told you," said Lizzie. "I want to be friends with my mom."

Miranda's expression of bewildered horror transformed into plain old shock. "Why?"

"Because *Orchids and Gumbo* made me realize that it's really important to spend time with your mother," said Lizzie simply.

Gordo gravely shook his head, as if Lizzie needed a reality check. "Parents scrape and sacrifice to provide us with shelter, support, and guidance," he explained, "and in return, we have as little to do with them as possible. It's nature's law."

"Yeah," agreed Miranda, frantically nodding. "It's like, you come home and they ask, 'What did you do today?' And we say, 'Nothing.' And they ask, 'Well, what are you doing tonight?' We say, 'I dunno.' And they ask, 'Why don't you ever talk to us?' And we say, 'Why can't you just leave me alone!' And you run upstairs."

Lizzie frowned.

"As little communication as possible," Gordo added. "It prepares us for marriage."

Hello? When are you guys going to grow up? GROW UP! GROW UP! GROW UP! GROW UP!

"Well, I want a more mature relationship with my mom," Lizzie told them. "I mean, she's already gone through all this stuff that I'm going through now—we can totally relate and support each other."

And, she can *drive.* That's a plus.

CHAPTER FIVE

"Your pot looks like an uncoordinated elephant seal," Mrs. McGuire teased.

"Well, *your* pot looks like an uncoordinated elephant seal *sat* on it," Lizzie teased right back.

Lizzie and her mother were perched behind pottery wheels, working big lumps of wet, gray clay. The day after Lizzie had run into her friends at the Digital Bean, she suggested that she and her mother take a pottery class together. Mrs. McGuire was totally all over it, so they'd gone right down to the Hillridge Craft Center and signed up.

"I've got something for you," said Mrs. McGuire in a serious tone.

Lizzie looked up expectantly—and her mother reached out and smeared wet clay on the tip of Lizzie's nose. "Mom!" squealed Lizzie. "Fine. I've got something for you, too. . . ."

Glancing around, Lizzie noticed a container of broken pieces of colored plastic for decorating pottery. She picked up a worthless red triangle and handed it to her mother. "Here."

"Oh!" Mrs. McGuire gushed as if Lizzie had just handed her a priceless ruby necklace. "It's a broken piece of pointy plastic! Thank you. I love it!"

"I really shopped around," said Lizzie, and they both started to laugh.

"Thanks for doing this with me," Lizzie told her mother. She pointed to the wet clay on her nose. "We learned a new craft *and* we got free facials."

Mrs. McGuire smiled. "This was a great idea you had, honey. But, you know what, I think I'm tired of making pots—I think I'm ready for a live, human model."

The two thought about that for a moment, then both exclaimed, "Denzel Washington!"

Just then, Mrs. McGuire's cell phone rang. With wet hands, she gingerly pulled it out of her pocket and answered. "Hello? . . . Oh, hi!"

As Mrs. McGuire listened to the person on the other end of the line, her smile slowly faded. "Again?" she said, her voice irritated. "No, I *do* take this seriously, but this keeps happening." After a sigh of frustration, she said, "You know what, I can't talk about this now. I'm throwing pots." She shook her head. "I'm not throwing them *at* anyone, I'm—it's what you call it when you make pots. I can't talk. I'm going to call you back later. Bye."

"What was that about?" asked Lizzie after her mother hung up.

"Nothing," said Mrs. McGuire.

But Lizzie knew she was lying. Her mother's fist started to mash the clay on her wheel with more force than necessary. Obviously, something was up. "C'mon, Mom, we're friends, now," Lizzie coaxed. "We can talk about stuff."

Mrs. McGuire thought it over. "Okay," she

said. "That was Nana. And she was telling me that she wants a separation from Grampa Chuck and that she's thinking of moving out."

Lizzie stopped breathing.

When I say, "You can tell me anything," I mean, "Too much information!"

"Nana?" squeaked Lizzie.

"She says she's missing out on life," explained Mrs. McGuire in exasperation. "She wants to go skiing in the Swiss Alps, then eat sushi in Tokyo, and—and go line dancing in Texas."

Lizzie's jaw dropped. She suddenly saw her eighty-year-old grandmother swishing down a hundred-meter ski-jump ramp, eating raw octopus with chopsticks, and line dancing in a Stetson and lizard-skin boots. Lizzie shuddered at the bizarre images flashing through her head.

Grandmothers are supposed to bake cookies and knit, thought Lizzie, not hang with Olympic skiers, sushi chefs, and cowboys.

"She says all Grampa Chuck wants to do is sit around all day and yell at the television set," Mrs. McGuire explained.

Yet another unnerving picture raced through Lizzie's mind. Grampa Chuck, a pale old man in a velour warm-up suit and enormous glasses, was springing out of his recliner to shake his fist at the TV and complain, "When did they cancel *Three's Company?*"

"They're getting separated?" Lizzie asked her mother.

Grandparents don't split up. Grandparents give you money when your parents aren't looking!

Mrs. McGuire shook her head and tried to reassure Lizzie. "She says this every year, and they have never split up. I'll go talk some sense into her, she'll go to Vegas for the weekend, and the whole thing will blow over.

"How come I've never heard about this before?" Lizzie asked.

"Oh, 'cause, I didn't want to worry you kids over nothing," said Lizzie's mom. "But, you know what, now that you and I are getting closer, it's nice having another woman to talk about it with."

Mrs. McGuire smiled, but Lizzie didn't.

"Yeah, it's great," she replied. And this time it was Lizzie who started pounding her clay with more force than necessary.

A few days later, Miranda called Gordo to update him on the situation with their best friend.

"So Lizzie's taking a pottery class with her mom, they're doing yoga, they even went horseback riding," she informed him.

"Hmm," said Gordo, kicking around his Hacky Sack. "Maybe it *is* possible to have fun hanging out with your parents."

"It does sound fun," Miranda admitted, twirling a lock of her hair. "It just seems . . . *weird.*"

"Yeah, well, there's lots of weird stuff in this world," Gordo pointed out. "Tofu bacon. Hairless cats. Country music."

"Yeah. Maybe Lizzie's onto something," Miranda said. "Maybe we should check it out, try hanging with *our* parents."

"I guess it's worth a try," agreed Gordo. "Can't be any weirder than tomato ice cream."

CHAPTER SIX

Meanwhile, back at the McGuire house, Matt and Lanny were totally immersed in the Great Chimp Hunt.

The two-foot-high primate kept showing up at the oddest times, causing all sorts of trouble. And Matt was determined to catch the hairy little animal and prove to his father, once and for all, that he hadn't been lying about the cause of all those nasty messes.

Matt figured the chimp was coming into

the house through the back door, so he and Lanny staked it out. Lanny waited just inside the house while Matt hid behind a wicker chair on the deck outside.

When the chimp finally scampered onto the deck's picnic table and lay down for a nap, Lanny crept from the house and Matt tiptoed out from behind the chair. But as the boys rushed forward to grab the chimp, he leaped off the table, and they crashed right into each other!

Next, Matt and Lanny tried hiding in the kitchen. Every time they heard the patter of little feet, they'd pop up from behind the counter to look. But by the time they did, the slippery chimp would always be gone!

As the days passed, they tried again and again—chasing the chimp upstairs, down-stairs, and around every tree in their back-yard. One day, they even dressed Matt up as a big banana. Matt sat quietly on the kitchen island, trying to lure the chimp, while Lanny hid behind him with a giant butterfly net. But the chimp was just too smart for them and refused to take the bait.

Finally, Matt and Lanny decided to hide in the trash cans near the backyard shed. Unfortunately, Mr. McGuire, who was oblivious to their stakeout, walked over. Without noticing the boys, he emptied a bag of kitchen garbage right into the can where Matt was hiding. As Matt's father strode back toward the house, Matt emerged from the trash can covered with tea bags, tissues, and rotten bits of vegetables. *Yuck!*

"This isn't working, Lanny," groaned Matt.

Lanny emerged from the garbage can next to Matt's and frowned at his muck-covered friend.

Matt sighed. "We need to catch this chimp

before he gets me grounded for life," he said. "We need some foolproof monkey bait."

Lanny nodded in total agreement, then he reached over to pull a lettuce leaf out of Matt's hair.

CHAPTER SEVEN

"**H**ey, Dad," said Gordo, approaching his father one afternoon. "I was wondering if maybe you wanted to go fishing this weekend. You know, just you and me."

Dr. Gordon looked up from his textbook. Behind his small, round glasses, his eyes focused on his son with grave concern. "Do you feel all right, David?" he asked.

"Yeah. Why?" asked Gordo.

"As a psychiatrist, I'm aware that you're at a

stage where it's normal for you to seek separation from your parents," he explained. "Yet, you appear to desire closeness, rather than distance."

Gordo shrugged. "Yeah, well, you never know what nutty thing I'll do next." He held up the book Mr. Dig had assigned the week before. "It's just, I've been reading *A River Runs Through It*, and it seems like it might be fun to go fishing."

Dr. Gordon nodded. He opened his day planner and looked over his busy schedule. "Ah, good luck!" Dr. Gordon said excitedly. "Saturday's wide open. We can leave at 6:30, breakfast at seven . . ." He scribbled the notations into his book. "Back on the road by 7:35; we can be at Inspiration Overlook by 8:15, where we can enjoy the majesty of nature for up to ten minutes. That leaves time for a spontaneous discussion of our place in the world and our emotional response to it. What do you think? Three minutes? Five minutes?"

Gordo grimaced at the thought of a heart-to-heart talk with his head-shrinking pop. "*Three* minutes," he insisted.

Meanwhile, over at the Sanchez house, Miranda was sitting on her bed doing some homework when her mother walked in.

"Hey, baby," said Mrs. Sanchez, holding out some folded laundry. "Here are some clean towels."

Miranda took them. "Hey, they smell 'springtime fresh,'" she said. "So, you want to be friends?"

"What?" asked Mrs. Sanchez.

"You know, I thought we could hang out, go to the mall or something," Miranda said with a shrug.

Mrs. Sanchez threw her hands in the air. "I'll get my purse!" she exclaimed.

"Really?" said Miranda. She couldn't believe it was such a big deal. Her mother was acting like she'd just won the lottery.

"Are you kidding?" said Mrs. Sanchez. "I get to spend *time* with my *daughter*? I'll even buy you a new outfit. And then you'll need some shoes to go with it. And then we can go eat, and then I'll take you to Baubles R Us and you can get some new makeup and some new things for your hair!" She paused and looked down at her housework overalls. "Oh! I've got to go get ready!"

Wow, thought Miranda, watching her mother race away. Who knew spending time with my mom would win *me* the lottery?

Back at the McGuire house, Lizzie and her mother were sitting at the kitchen table, coating their misshapen pottery creations with an array of acrylic colors.

"I'm still a little worried about your nana," Mrs. McGuire admitted to Lizzie as she brushed some red paint on the kiln-fired vase. "She went to Vegas like she always does when she's upset, but this time, when she came back, she was still unhappy with Grampa Chuck. And she'd won *four* bingo jackpots."

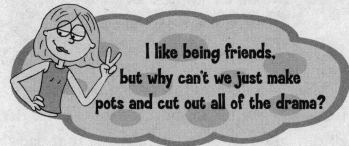

I like being friends, but why can't we just make pots and cut out all of the drama?

"I guess it's just one of those times when you have to wait and see how it all turns out," Mrs. McGuire continued. "Like we did when your dad had that big tax problem."

Lizzie froze, her paintbrush hanging in

midair. "Dad had tax problems?" she asked with dread.

"Oh, *yeah*," said Mrs. McGuire, blithely painting away. "The government said we owed them a lot of money. I mean, we thought we were going to lose the house, everything."

No more! No more! Wa-wa-wa! Wa-wa-wa! I can't hear you! Woo-oo! Woo-oo!

Mrs. McGuire didn't notice how freaked Lizzie was getting, so she just kept talking. "It all turned out to be a big mistake. Your dad's Social Security number is one digit different from Bill Gates's. So that explains why the government thought we owed them six hundred and eighteen million dollars."

Lizzie grimaced. She suddenly saw her poor

father, working all night at his adding machine, trying to add up columns of numbers, but never coming close to figuring out how to pay his taxes. She saw her family packing up their house and moving into a tent, the police coming to haul her parents off to jail, and herself and Matt on the run, hitchhiking to Mexico.

Lizzie shook her head clear of the disturbing visions. Whoa, she thought, if I keep sitting here, my mom's going to tell me even more horror stories. I can't handle this!

"Omigosh, I just remembered!" Lizzie blurted out. "I have, like, a ton of homework. It's going to take me hours."

"Do you need help?" asked Mrs. McGuire.

"I think I better do this on my own," said Lizzie quickly. "I mean, how else am I going to learn? Bye!"

Then Lizzie was *so outie*!

Later that day, Lizzie's father walked through the front door and spotted a bunch of bananas just sitting in the middle of the entryway.

That's odd, he thought.

He studied the fruit, wondering who had left it there. Then he leaned over to pick it up. The moment he did, he noticed a string had been tied to the bananas.

Odder still, he thought.

The string was wrapped around a candle in the living room, and when he'd picked up the bananas, he'd also pulled the string, which jerked the candle off the mantel.

Fascinated by the chain reaction, Mr. McGuire continued to watch as the candle fell onto the pedal of a batting tee, which shot up a blast of air, dislodging a ball at the top. The ball fell onto a remote control, which turned on a radio-controlled race car, which raced across the floor to a jack-in-the-box.

When the car hit the jack-in-the-box, it popped open, and the swinging lid struck the toggle switch of a desk lamp, which turned it on. The light of the lamp was positioned to shine through a magnifying glass, which made it burn through a piece of strategically positioned string. When the string broke, it released a heavy boot, which hung on a pendulum-like hinge from the ceiling.

The boot swung down, kicking a bowling ball at one end of a shelf. The ball rolled off the shelf and landed on one end of a seesaw, which dislodged an enormous sack of rice. The rice plummeted from the top of the TV cabinet, causing a noose to tighten around Mr. McGuire's ankles and jerk him feetfirst into the air.

"Yarrrghh! What?" cried Mr. McGuire as he found himself dangling from the ceiling.

He couldn't believe he'd been duped. But the elaborate mousetrap had been so mesmerizing, he'd never considered that *he* might be the mouse!

Knowing there was only one person in the McGuire house with a mind twisted enough to set up this evil mechanism, Mr. McGuire opened his mouth and bellowed, "Matt! *Matt*!"

A moment later, a chimp scampered into view. Mr. McGuire yelped, startled by the hairy little beast. "All right," murmured Mr. McGuire in astonishment. "So there *is* a monkey."

The chimp snatched away the bananas, then pointed at Mr. McGuire and let loose with a nasty, mocking laugh.

"Hey, give me those bananas!" cried Mr. McGuire as the chimp turned and raced for the door. "Matt! Hey, Matt!"

Mr. McGuire watched as a green blanket was thrown over the chimp.

"Good toss, Lanny!" cried Matt. Then he raced up to his father and said, "It's okay, Dad, we got him. Lanny was right—he knew that if you got caught in our banana trap, the chimp couldn't resist coming out and laughing at you."

Mr. McGuire sighed. He had to admit that Matt and Lanny had, without a doubt, proven their innocence. "Yeah, son," he said, "the next time you tell me there's a chimp loose in the house, I'm going to believe you. I'm sorry. You know, I think we all learned a lot from this."

"Yup," said Matt. "You've learned to trust me more, and I've learned that you make *great* monkey bait."

CHAPTER EIGHT

Later that evening, Lizzie was dejectedly sipping a glass of iced tea on the back deck.

"Lizzie? You out there?" called Mrs. McGuire.

Lizzie sighed. She'd been hiding from her mother all evening. Now she was busted. "Uh-huh," she said.

Ah, man. She tracked me down.

"Well, I just talked to Nana," said Mrs. McGuire, sitting down next to Lizzie on the porch swing.

Please, no more grown-up stuff! No more! No more!

"Grampa Chuck bought her a single red rose and took her out for Mongolian barbecue," continued Mrs. McGuire. "Everything's fine. All she needed was a night out with her husband."

Phew!

"Honey, I can't tell you how great it has been having you to talk all of this out with," said Mrs. McGuire.

"Yeah, it's been great, Mom," said Lizzie dully. "You're welcome."

Mrs. McGuire heard the unease in Lizzie's voice. Her brow furrowed with concern. "Is everything okay?" she asked.

"Yeah. Everything's fine. I mean, Nana and Grampa Chuck are back together, so it's all good," said Lizzie. She shrugged. "I guess I freaked out for no reason."

"You freaked out?" asked Lizzie's mother.

"No," said Lizzie quickly. She didn't want her mother to know she couldn't handle this stuff. Then she frowned, realizing that maybe she *did* want her to know. With a sigh, she finally told her mother the truth.

"I did freak out," Lizzie admitted. "I didn't want to, Mom—I wanted to be there for you. But . . . Nana and Grampa Chuck were splitting up. Dad was having tax problems and I . . ."

Mrs. McGuire sighed. "Honey, I'm really sorry," she said. "I really didn't want to upset you."

"I know," said Lizzie. "But I *did* get upset. So maybe I'm just not ready for this sort of thing yet."

The kind of stuff I'm ready for is: "How do I get Ethan Craft to like me?" and "Am I having a good hair day?" ... And I'm barely ready for *that*!

"I *like* doing stuff together, Mom," she said, "and feeling like I can share things with you. But maybe we'll just have to wait for a few years. Is that okay?"

Lizzie's mother smiled. "Sure," she said, then added, "I'm going to miss you, sweet potato."

"I'm going to miss you, too, Mom," said Lizzie. "But I'm glad to know that we *can* be friends."

"So am I. And I know it's going to be worth the wait," said Mrs. McGuire, reaching into her pocket. "Why don't you hang onto this until then—" She handed Lizzie the piece of red plastic from their day of making pottery.

"Oh? It's your pointy hunk of broken plastic," said Lizzie in a teasing tone.

"And it's very, very precious to me," said Mrs. McGuire sincerely. "So you can give it back to me when we're ready to be friends. Okay?"

Lizzie nodded. "Okay."

Then they gave each other an Orchids-and-Gumbo-Poker-Club hug—and Lizzie realized they'd even done it out on the "veranda" . . . just like Tallulah and Darcy Lou.

Ding-dong!

Inside the house, the doorbell rang, and

Mr. McGuire got up from the sofa to answer it. Matt and Lanny followed him, leading the chimp out of the living room by a leash.

As Mr. McGuire greeted the two men at the door, Matt knelt in front of the chimp and told him, "I just want you to know that you're an evil demon-chimp and I never want to see your evil face again."

Lanny nodded in total agreement.

"Hi," said a scruffy-looking guy at the door, "you called about our chimp?"

"Yeah," said Mr. McGuire. The guy's name was David. He and Mr. McGuire played on the same softball team, and Mr. McGuire remembered he'd said something about having a pet chimp.

"There you are, Fredo!" David exclaimed, opening his arms to his pet. The chimp ran right to him. "I am so glad you found him. He is such a little sweetheart, isn't he?"

Matt narrowed his eyes at that remark, then reminded himself—if you can't say anything *nice*, better not to say anything at all.

"Time to go home," said the other man, whose name was Jeremy.

"I missed you," blubbered David.

"I know you ran off, Fredo," said Jeremy. "You broke my heart."

Then David and Jeremy each took one of Fredo's hairy little hands and turned to leave.

"So," said David to his buddies, "Chinese food tonight?"

As they left, the chimp turned to Matt and gave him one last raspberry. Good riddance, thought Matt and Lanny, and they gave him one right back!

A few days later, Miranda was hanging with Gordo at the Digital Bean's counter.

" . . . And then she bought me these new

earrings, and five things of lip gloss, and a really cool sweater," said Miranda.

"And yet you don't seem too happy," Gordo observed.

Miranda shrugged. "Well, she was so happy I spent time with her that she was going to buy me everything in the mall. I felt so guilty."

"Bad time for your conscience to kick in," said Gordo.

"Tell me about it," agreed Miranda with a sigh. Then she remembered that Gordo had also engaged in a close encounter of the parental kind. "Oh, so, how was the fishing?"

"Didn't happen," said Gordo flatly. "During our 8:15 appreciation of the majesty of nature, we were the target of an unscheduled skunk attack. I spent the entire day bathing in tomato juice."

Miranda leaned toward him and cautiously

sniffed. "You smell like a, a pine tree," she said.

"That's because I'm wearing a car air freshener," he said, pulling up a string hanging around his neck. A green cardboard air freshener in the shape of a pine tree emerged from under his shirt.

"Hey, you guys," called Lizzie, striding up to them.

"Hey," said Gordo. He noticed Lizzie's mother was with her. *Again.* "Hey, Mrs. McGuire."

"So, I'm going to see you at home later?" Mrs. McGuire asked Lizzie.

"You're not staying?" asked Miranda, unable to keep the hopefulness that Mrs. McGuire would leave out of her voice.

"No," she said. "I'm just dropping Lizzie off and getting some coffee to go." Then she headed toward the register at the end of the counter, pausing only for a moment to wrinkle her nose at Gordo and wonder why he smelled like a pine forest.

"So, why aren't you hanging out with your mom?" asked Miranda.

Lizzie shrugged. "I think things just didn't work out."

Miranda nodded knowingly. "It's tough hanging out with parents," she said.

"They have their world, and we have ours," said Gordo in one of his typically pithy summations. "It's a bad idea to mix them."

"Yeah. Bad idea," Lizzie agreed.

But was it really? she wondered as she fingered the broken piece of plastic now dangling from her charm bracelet. The Orchids and Gumbo Poker Club wasn't exactly a *total* failure, Lizzie decided. After all, she and her mother now had some special memories.

Across the room, Mrs. McGuire had gotten

her coffee and was about to leave. When she glanced back in Lizzie's direction, mother and daughter shared one last private smile.

It was then that Lizzie knew exactly what they would say to each other when she finally felt ready to return that little piece of plastic. . . .

"*Oh, Momma, Momma. I want us to be friends! Friends forever.*"

And her mother would turn back to her, and say in a voice as sugary as a Louisiana praline:

"*Oh, I'm so glad, sweet potato. And I can finally say it—welcome to the Orchids and Gumbo Poker Club.*"

PART TWO

CHAPTER ONE

After they had collected their smoothies from the counter at the Digital Bean, Miranda Sanchez challenged her two best friends, Lizzie McGuire and David "Gordo" Gordon, to admit their most embarrassing moments.

"Okay. My most embarrassing moment," said Lizzie, heading for a corner table, "was when I was in front of the class working a problem. I dropped my chalk, and when I bent over to pick it up . . ." Lizzie's voice trailed off as she recalled the sound of her pants ripping.

"Oh, I remember that!" cried Miranda, as she and Lizzie sat down. "Your underwear said Tuesday when it was really Wednesday!"

Lizzie cringed at the memory.

"I can top that," said Gordo, pulling a chair up next to the girls. "The first and last time I went bowling, I threw nine straight gutter balls in a row. I got so tense that my fingers started to swell up and . . . well . . ." He shuddered, remembering the horrible sound of that emergency room chain saw. "They had to surgically remove the ball."

"You think that's bad?" said Miranda. "In the holiday pageant—"

Just then, Lizzie noticed Ethan Craft walking up to their table. Lizzie made a silent "cut it" motion, but Miranda didn't seem to notice. She just kept talking.

"I was one of the Eight Maids a-Milkin'," she babbled, "and I accidentally *threw up* on one of the Ten Lords a-Leapin'!" For effect, she pretended to throw up all over the Digital Bean table. "That was *definitely* my most embarrassing moment." Then she noticed Ethan standing behind her. "Oh," she groaned in total humiliation, "until now."

"Hey, don't sweat it, Miranda," said Ethan.

Too late. Miranda's cheeks had already turned fire-engine red.

Ethan shrugged and patted her shoulder. "The holidays are tough on everyone," he noted, then he shot Lizzie and Gordo a grin. "Hey, what's up, guys?"

"Hey, Ethan," said Lizzie with a dreamy smile. Gordo shrugged a halfhearted hello, and Miranda darted away, back to the café counter in embarrassment.

"Yo, Gor-don," said Ethan. "Remember

the movie you told me to rent last weekend? It totally rocked. You're like my own little critic, dude."

Hey! I want to be his little, uh . . . *something*!

"Yeah, well," said Gordo, "Friday night, they're showing *Psycho* down at the Wilco. Now, *that's* a classic."

"That's in black and white, right?" said Ethan.

Gordo nodded.

"See, I'm more of a color type of guy," Ethan declared.

Awww . . . He likes color. I wear color. . . . We're *made* for each other!

Gordo let out a sigh. In his experience, whether the subject was classic movies or algebra, educating Ethan was a futile endeavor.

"Besides," said Ethan, "me and some friends are going bowling Friday night."

"Oh, really," said Miranda, returning to their table with a newly purchased big cookie—and her cheeks back to a relatively normal color. "That's a coincidence, 'cause *we're* going bowling on Friday night, too."

"We are?" Lizzie asked, shooting Miranda a confused look. Miranda responded with a look of her own—one that said *duh*!

Lizzie gulped. "Oh, right," she said quickly. "We *are*."

I love Miranda. She thinks of everything.

"Coolness," said Ethan. "We'll hang." He turned to Gordo. "I'll bet you're like an ace with the pins, too, right? Like, what *can't* you do?"

Gordo grimaced at the implication that he excelled at everything, but Ethan didn't notice. He just tossed the gang at the table one of his easygoing Ethan waves and said, "Later."

Lizzie waited until Ethan had stepped away, then she exploded. "Can you believe that we're going bowling with Ethan Craft?"

"We're going to have so much fun!" cried Miranda.

"Were you guys not listening?" asked Gordo in a seriously annoyed tone. "There is no way I'm having another bowling ball surgically removed from one of my hands. . . . Have fun."

"But we just told Ethan we'd be there," wailed Miranda.

Gordo rolled his eyes. "Oh, and I don't want to disappoint him," he cracked.

Miranda frowned at Gordo's sarcasm, but Lizzie remained oblivious. "I cannot believe this!" she exclaimed. "Do you know what this means?"

It means I am going to marry Ethan Craft! . . . Hey, you've got to start somewhere.

Miranda turned to Lizzie—and both girls let out an ear-piercing shriek of excitement.

Gordo, of course, just covered his ears.

CHAPTER TWO

Later that afternoon, Lizzie and Miranda talked on the phone nonstop about their group date with Ethan Craft.

"Omigosh, I still can't believe it," said Lizzie as she raced into the kitchen to grab her microwave popcorn. "Omigosh, I know! . . . Omigosh, he is! . . ."

Lizzie never even noticed her dad observing her. She was too caught up in the dozens of crucial decisions that needed to be made before the weekend—shoes, clothes, hair, bag, gloss!

"Did you hear that?" Mr. McGuire asked his wife, after Lizzie raced out of the kitchen and back up to her bedroom.

"Hear what?" asked Mrs. McGuire, chopping vegetables at the kitchen counter.

"Lizzie, just now on the phone," said Mr. McGuire, trying to twist the cap off a sticky bottle of old salad dressing. "Apparently, she's very excited about something. The rest of it, I don't know. . . . I don't even know *her* anymore." He finally managed to open the bottle. He brought the cap to his nose, trying to determine whether or not the contents had gone bad. "Do you remember when she used to want to spend time with us?"

"That was before she was embarrassed to be seen with us," said Mrs. McGuire. She stopped chopping vegetables and looked up to find her husband sniffing the salad dressing cap.

"I had no idea we were embarrassing," he said. He pulled the bottle cap away from his face—and left a dollop of salad dressing on his nose.

"*I'm* not," said Mrs. McGuire with a raised eyebrow.

Mr. McGuire just kept staring at his wife, completely unaware that the tip of his nose was now the flavor of garlic-pepper ranch.

"Honey, it's the age," Mrs. McGuire told her husband as she walked over with a hand towel and wiped down her husband's nose. "Come on. She thinks the only reason we live here is to make her life miserable."

"But she's growing up so fast," said Mr. McGuire. "I want to be a part of her life. . . . You know what I'm going to do? I'm going to have dinner this weekend with Lizzie. Just the two of us."

"Oh, that's very sweet," said Mrs. McGuire. She could see that this gesture was very important to her husband, although she wasn't sure Lizzie would see it the same way.

"No, it'll be great," insisted Mr. McGuire. "I mean, all I've got to do is show her I can be 'down.' I mean, I am 'right . . . on.' With the kids. And I am the real 'Sam Shady.'"

Mrs. McGuire cringed at her husband's attempt to use street lingo. "Honey, now you're embarrassing *me*," she told him.

While Mr. and Mrs. McGuire were in the kitchen discussing their problems, Lizzie's brother, Matt, and his always-quiet friend, Lanny, were sitting on the living room couch.

"I'm getting pretty sick of Heywood Briggs bullying us around," Matt told his best friend.

Lanny nodded and tightened the blanket wrapped around him.

"And I'm getting pretty tired of him using us as footballs," continued Matt. "I mean, sure it's fun flying through the air like that, but landing's a little rough."

He pointed to the blanket wrapped around Lanny. "And why'd he have to go and take your clothes? There was already a flag waving from the flagpole."

Poor Lanny had been forced to hide behind the school sign until Matt brought him a blanket from the school nurse's office. Thanks to Heywood, Lanny's pants and shirt were now flying over their elementary school instead of the Stars and Stripes.

"For the first time in my life, I don't have a plan," admitted Matt, shaking his head.

Suddenly, Lanny raised his eyebrows.

"Really?" said Matt. "You think that

working out until we're bigger than Heywood will work?"

Lanny's face brightened.

"Well, come on," said Matt confidently. "Let's go see if we have any dumbbells lying around."

As they left the room, Lanny smiled and Matt laughed.

"That's a good one," Matt said. "Lizzie probably *is* in her room. . . . You crack me up."

After dinner that evening, Lizzie was back in the kitchen, grabbing a scoop of ice cream. Her dad walked in and cleared his throat.

"Hey, Lizzie," he said.

"Yo, Dad," said Lizzie.

He bobbed his head. "What's *the hap?*"

Lizzie's brow furrowed. She tossed the ice cream container back in the freezer and went to the silverware drawer for a spoon. "The hap?" she repeated, hoping her hearing was off and she *hadn't* just heard her dad make a totally lame attempt to use hip-hop slang.

"Yeah, you know, I'm just *checkin'* it with you," said Mr. McGuire.

Omigosh, thought Lizzie in horror, he's trying to be hip. I'd better nip this middle-aged rapper delusion thing in the bud. "*Checkin'* what?" she said pointedly. "What are you *talking* about?" Then the lightbulb went off. "Wait, you've been reading one of those 'How to Talk to Your Kids' books again, haven't you?"

Mr. McGuire's face fell. "No," he said. "But there is something I'd like to ask you."

Lizzie's whole body tensed with dread.

Okay, that's never good. . . . But whatever it is, I'm sure I can blame it on Matt.

"Sure," Lizzie asked uneasily, "what's up?"

Mr. McGuire crossed and uncrossed his arms uncomfortably. "Well," he said, "I was wondering. . . . Would you like to have dinner together Friday night?"

"Uh, well, don't we have dinner together, like, *every* night?" said Lizzie.

"Well, yeah," replied Mr. McGuire, "but I'm talking just the two of us. You know, like a daddy-daughter date night."

Lizzie bit her cheek to keep from laughing out loud.

Daddy-daughter date night? He is *definitely* reading one of those books!

"Um, sure, I guess so," said Lizzie, trying hard to keep a straight face. "It'll be . . . fun."

"Fun. Exactly! Just what I thought," said Mr. McGuire. "You know, like, cool . . . lio." He held up a fist in solidarity as he edged out of the kitchen. Lizzie gamely tried to copy the gesture. Then she shook her head and sighed. My poor, pathetic, clueless father, she thought. Gotta give him karma points for trying!

CHAPTER THREE

At lunch the next day, Miranda walked up to Gordo. He was sitting at an outdoor table, reading a book.

"Hey," she said, setting her tray down and dropping into the seat across from him.

Gordo's head jerked up, and he hid the book he was reading below the table. "Hey, what's up?" he said tensely.

Miranda stared at him. "Why are you turning red?" she asked. Then she narrowed her eyes in suspicion. "What's in that book?"

Gordo's expression went from uneasy to completely panicked—and Miranda suddenly changed her mind. "No, don't answer," she told him quickly. "I probably don't even want to know." Knowing Gordo, she thought, it's probably something totally gross, like a book about cadaver dissection.

Gordo sighed and brought the book out of hiding. Miranda read the title and author aloud. "*The Dude Strikes Out*, by Jeffrey Lebowski." She shook her head in confusion. "You're reading a book about bowling? I thought you weren't going with us anyway."

"Well, I wasn't. But then I decided that it might be good for me," Gordo admitted.

"Why?" asked Miranda.

"Because I don't want to be limited by my fears," Gordo replied sincerely.

"Huh?" asked Miranda. In her mind, fear was an emotion reserved for stuff like skydiving, bungee jumping, and snorkeling in shark-infested waters. Not *bowling*. Not ever.

"Look," Gordo explained, "you still perform in holiday pageants without throwing up. Lizzie can do math problems without ripping her pants. I should be able to bowl without having to go to the emergency room."

Miranda nodded. When he put it like that, she totally understood. "You're right," she told him. "One miserable experience shouldn't ruin all the rest. . . . I'll help you. I'll be your life coach."

"I don't need a life coach," said Gordo. "I just need to learn to bowl." He put his nose back in the book.

"Gordo. *Bowling* isn't the problem," said

Miranda, plucking the book from his hands. She knew exactly how to help. A few months back, she'd watched a TV psychologist use behavior-changing techniques on audience volunteers, and she was *sure* she could use the same methods on Gordo.

"I'm going to teach you to relax," Miranda told him, "so even if you throw a few gutter balls, they won't need to get the bowling ball off your hand with a hammer."

"Well, they actually use a saw," he informed her. "But I get your point."

"So you're in?" asked Miranda.

Gordo bit his lip, considering it, then said, "Okay."

"Wow," said Miranda, "I can't believe I get to help *you*." Gordo was usually the guy with all the answers—the one who thought of solutions to everyone else's problems. "Now, *this* is a first."

"Believe me," said Gordo, "there's no one more surprised than me."

Later that day, Lizzie was hanging in the hall outside her English classroom when she noticed one of her favorite substitute teachers striding toward the door.

"Hey, Mr. Dig," she called.

Mr. Dig stopped in front of Lizzie and removed his bright yellow portable CD earphones.

"I didn't know we had a sub for English today," Lizzie told him.

"Well," he said with a raised eyebrow, "you know what else you don't know? What you'll be having for breakfast tomorrow morning, what you'll be doing after school next Thursday, and who you'll be going to the senior prom with. . . . Life's interesting that way, don't you think?"

Lizzie looked puzzled.

Just when I think I'm happy to see him, Mr. Dig has to go and get all mind-gamey on me.

"Yeah, sure," said Lizzie.

Mr. Dig smiled and ducked inside the classroom just as Gordo and Miranda arrived.

"Oh, hey, guys," she said. She'd been at the dentist's office all morning, and this was the first chance she had to consult with them about her father's bizarro behavior. "My dad is being so weird. He wants to have dinner with me this weekend."

Miranda frowned in confusion. "Don't you have dinner with him every night?" she asked.

Gordo shook his head. "Well, me bowling on Friday night is pretty much guaranteed to be worse than your dinner on Saturday," he assured her.

"Gordo," said Miranda in a critical tone.

Gordo exchanged a look with her. Then he sighed and chanted, "Bowling is fun. Bowling is good. Bowling will not make my fingers swell."

Miranda smiled, reached into a foil package, and handed Gordo a chocolate cookie. "Good boy," she said, then patted his head.

Gordo chewed—and resisted the urge to bark.

"Wait a minute. Did you just say that bowling was on Friday night?" asked Lizzie, ignoring the totally weird exchange she'd just witnessed. "I thought it was Saturday."

"No, it's Friday," said Miranda, pointing to her head. "Burned on my brain."

"But that's when I said I'd have dinner with my dad!" cried Lizzie.

"Well, how 'bout *I* have dinner with your

dad and *you* go bowling for me?" suggested Gordo.

"Gordo!" snapped Miranda. Once again, her critical look reminded him that negative thoughts about bowling were *not* productive.

Gordo sighed. "Bowling is fun. Bowling is good. Bowling will not make my fingers swell," he chanted.

Miranda handed Gordo another cookie, which he promptly ate.

"Well, you can't *not* go," Miranda told Lizzie. "Ethan's going to be there!"

Lizzie rolled her eyes. "Thanks for reminding me." Like I could forget, she thought.

"So what are you going to do?" asked Gordo. "Who are you going to spend Friday night with?"

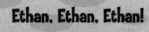

Ethan, Ethan, Ethan!

"Cancel with my dad of course. What else am I supposed to do? It'll be fine. He'll totally understand," said Lizzie with certainty.

Just then, the late bell rang. Miranda and Gordo headed to class, but for some reason, Lizzie couldn't get her legs to move.

I'm totally doing the right thing, she assured herself, standing alone in the empty hallway. "I think," she muttered.

CHAPTER FOUR

Meanwhile, Matt and Lanny had dived right into their Get-Bigger-Than-Heywood-Briggs fitness plan.

Because they'd need lots of internal fuel to pump iron, Phase One consisted of stuffing themselves with protein bars and energy shakes. Then they were ready for Phase Two.

The two boys changed into workout clothing, and Matt sat down on the floor. He and Lanny argued about how many sit-ups would constitute a good first effort. They settled on an even hundred.

Finally, Lanny held Matt's ankles, and Matt began to exercise. His effort was tremendous. He began to feel sweaty and breathless. "How many sit-ups is that?" he asked between gasps of air.

Lanny held up four fingers.

"This isn't working," said Matt. This fitness thing takes way too much effort! Clearly, they needed a new plan.

"Hey!" Matt cried after considering alternatives. "*Invisibility.* You can't bully what you can't see. Let's go!"

To test their invisibility plan, the boys painted themselves the exact same shade as the eggshell white wall along the staircase. Then they flattened themselves against it and waited for someone to walk by and *not* notice them.

When Mr. McGuire headed down the

staircase, thumbing through a restaurant guidebook, Matt and Lanny closed their eyes and held their breath.

"Hey, Lanny. Hey, Matt," said Mr. McGuire as he strolled by.

"Doh!" Matt groaned, smacking his head in frustration. So much for invisibility!

Mr. McGuire just kept walking and thumbing through his restaurant guide. He was intensely searching for the perfect restaurant to take Lizzie to on Friday.

"Oh, hey, Lizzie," he called, walking into the family living room. "I was wondering, how does Indian food sound to you?"

Lizzie looked up from the carpet, where she was doing her homework. "Um . . ." she stalled.

Uh-oh. He's actually picking out some fancy restaurant. The kind where they serve ketchup on a plate.

"I just thought it'd be kind of fun for you and me to try some new kind of cuisine together," said her father.

Okay, I'll break it to him easy.

Mr. McGuire scratched his head. He could see his daughter was uneasy for some reason. He thought it might be the restaurant choice. "I'm happy to keep it simple if you want burgers and pizza," he said quickly. "I'm A-OK with that."

Oh, no. He's making this difficult!

Lizzie took a deep breath and tried to

choose her words carefully. "Dad, I've given this a lot of thought," she said slowly, "and . . . maybe we could reschedule."

Mr. McGuire's face fell. "Oh," he said. The disappointment was hard to miss.

"It's just because, me, Gordo, and Miranda were planning on going bowling this weekend," Lizzie swiftly explained. "And some other people from school are going and it's sort of turning into this big . . . thing."

"Lizzie, I understand," said Mr. McGuire, doing his best to hide his hurt feelings. "Go bowling with your friends. Have a good time."

Wow. Dad's actually being cool. Without even trying!

Lizzie smiled. She could see her dad was a little disappointed, but she was sure he understood. "Dad, I know when we can spend some time together," she suggested, rising from the floor and gathering her homework.

"When?" he asked, his face brightening.

"You could drive me to the bowling alley," said Lizzie, putting a hand on his shoulder. "It's, like, a *ten-minute* drive. Tons of time to talk."

Once again, Mr. McGuire swallowed his disappointment. "That's . . . great," he told Lizzie. "Count me in."

"Thanks for understanding, Dad," she said. Then she kissed his cheek and raced up to her bedroom, leaving her disappointed father behind.

The next day, Gordo and his "life coach" met up for yet another behavior-changing session in the school's outdoor quad.

"Bowling is fun. Bowling is good. Bowling will not make my fingers swell," Gordo chanted.

"Oh, excellent!" cried Miranda, handing him his reinforcement cookie. "I think we're ready for Phase Two."

"Does Phase Two involve cookies?" asked Gordo hopefully.

Miranda frowned. "Sit down," she commanded, pointing to a bench. They both took a load off. "Okay," she said, "now close your eyes."

Gordo nodded and obeyed.

"Now visualize a bowling alley," Miranda instructed.

"Okay," he said.

"Now. Be the ball," she told him.

Gordo opened his eyes. "*Be* the ball?" he asked skeptically.

"Be the ball," she repeated in the sort of

singsong Zen voice Gordo usually heard in martial-arts movies.

With a sigh, he closed his eyes and gave it a try. In his mind he visualized himself as a bowling ball. Suddenly, he was thrown down the polished boards of a bowling alley, careening toward the set of pins at the other end—and crashing headfirst into them!

"Aah!" cried Gordo, opening his eyes in terror. He vigorously shook his head. "I don't want to be the ball!"

"Okay," said Miranda in a calming voice. "Then be the pins."

Gordo tried again. He closed his eyes and visualized himself standing at the far end of a bowling alley. A collection of white pins was lined up in a nice, neat triangle behind him. Okay, he thought, I'm the lead pin, pretty good so far.

Suddenly, he heard a rumble like thunder.

Someone had thrown a ball at the other end of the alley. The ball was huge. The size of a boulder. And it was rolling right for him!

"Aah!" cried Gordo as the boulder ball smashed into him and sent him flying. Once again, Gordo's eyes flew open in terror. "Being the pins isn't working either," he told Miranda.

Just then, Mr. Dig glided by them on his scooter—and crashed right into a tree in the middle of the quad. Miranda and Gordo rushed to his side.

"Mr. Dig, are you okay?" Miranda cried.

"Mr. Dig, what happened?" asked Gordo.

Their favorite substitute teacher blinked, then grinned. "I crashed!" he said with absolute glee.

"Yeah. You did," said Miranda, sharing a concerned look with Gordo. Jolly enthusiasm was *not* your typical response to an embarrassing wipeout. But then again, thought Miranda, Mr. Dig was not your typical teacher.

"It was just a matter of time," Mr. Dig told them. He tapped his helmet. "But I came prepared. Woo-hoo, that felt good!"

Gordo turned to Miranda. "You think he's got a concussion?" he asked quietly. "He's making less sense than normal."

Mr. Dig stood up and brushed himself off. "Look, y'all, I'm fine, really," he said. "That was kind of fun."

"But you totally wiped out," Gordo said.

"Yup. And that's never happened to me before," said the teacher. "I love new experiences!"

"Mr. Dig," said Miranda, "you're kind of freaky."

Mr. Dig shrugged. "Well, it's all part of the journey," he told her.

Gordo rolled his eyes. "Let me guess. Life's journey?" he asked.

"No," said Mr. Dig, "the journey to the attendance office." He hoisted his scooter over his shoulder and turned toward the school building. "But I like the way you're thinking, Gordo."

Gordo shook his head, watching Mr. Dig walk away. "I don't get it," he told Miranda. "The guy eats dirt and he still has a smile on his face."

Miranda shrugged. "Like I said, freaky."

CHAPTER FIVE

"Target is approaching," Matt whispered into his walkie-talkie. "I repeat, target is approaching. Over."

Across the room, Lanny nodded. The two boys had come up with yet another plan to defeat the bully Heywood Briggs. This particular scheme involved combat fatigues and camouflage face paint—as well as plastic wrap and a whole lot of honey.

Each boy had taken up a stakeout position

to get the drop on their target. Lanny was crouched behind the kitchen island, and Matt was hanging back behind a potted plant in the adjoining family room.

"Prepare for Operation Mummy," Matt whispered into his walkie-talkie. "Over."

Because they wanted to be certain their scheme would work on Heywood, the boys agreed to run a preliminary test—on Lizzie.

Without a clue that she was being set up, Lizzie walked down the stairs and across the open space between the kitchen and the family room. Suddenly, she stopped. Something sticky was holding her pink boots to the floor—her *favorite* pair of faux lizard-skin boots.

She looked down to find the soles mired in a gooey puddle of honey! In outrage, she pulled at her boots, trying to work them free.

Just then, she heard Matt begin to shout like an army drill sergeant.

"Move, move, move!" Matt barked as he and Lanny flew out of their hiding places and raced toward Lizzie.

"What?" she cried in confusion.

Using an entire box of plastic wrap, Matt and Lanny began to wrap Lizzie like an Egyptian mummy, pinning her arms to her sides. "You're not so tough now, are you, Heywood!" cried Matt.

"Heywood?" Lizzie cried, totally confused.

The boys kept circling Lizzie. Faster and faster they circled until *Bam!* Matt ran right into Lanny, and they both fell to the floor.

"Matt! Unwrap me!" Lizzie demanded.

Matt held his head. "I will, I will," he said, trying to focus on his sister. But the whole room looked like it was spinning, including

Lizzie. "Could you just *stay still* a second?" Matt said.

"I can't move, you ignoramus!" Lizzie snapped.

Matt shook his head clear. He looked at his sister again. "What did you say?" he asked with desperate hope in his voice.

"I said I can't move!" she shouted.

Matt tossed Lanny a victorious look. "Mission accomplished," he declared with a grin. "But for Heywood, though, we'll need to double our supplies."

"If you don't unwrap me this second, I'm gonna call Mom," Lizzie threatened.

Matt and Lanny jumped to their feet. "No, no, no, don't do that," insisted Matt.

"Fine, I won't call Mom," said Lizzie.

Matt sighed, relieved. But when the boys took their good old time giving each other a complicated high-five handshake, she changed her mind.

"M-o-o-o-o-o-o-m!" she yelled.

Matt and Lanny scampered away, looking for cover.

Fifteen minutes later, Mrs. McGuire was sitting on Lizzie's bed, using expensive cleaning fluid and a special cloth to get the honey off Lizzie's favorite footwear.

Lizzie sat in the corner scowling. "Why isn't Matt the one cleaning my boots?" she huffed.

"Would you really trust your brother with this job?" asked her mother as she delicately wiped the faux lizard-skin surface.

Lizzie's scowl deepened.

"I didn't think so," said her mother.

"Still," said Lizzie, "he ruins everything. I was going to wear these tomorrow, Mom."

The boots were the *only* item of clothing

she'd actually made a decision on—every other fashion choice she'd been agonizing over for days. But Lizzie refused to be discouraged. It wasn't every day a girl had to select just the right outfit to inspire Ethan Craft to propose marriage to her.

"Well, honey, you're still going to have to take your boots off to go bowling," Mrs. McGuire pointed out.

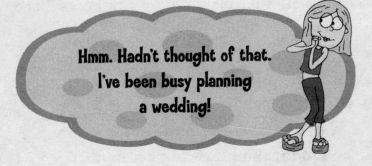

Lizzie went to her closet and took out a collection of pants, skirts, and tops. It had taken her days to narrow her choices down to six possible ensembles.

I am *so* close, she thought.

"So your dad told me you canceled your plans with him," said Mrs. McGuire.

"Yeah," she told her mother as she critically eyed a pink sparkle tank and gauzy blouse combination. "But he understands why, right?"

"Oh, yeah," said Mrs. McGuire. "Your dad knows you'd *rather* spend the time with your *friends.*"

Lizzie frowned, not liking the way her mother put it. "It's just that me, Gordo, and Miranda usually spend Fridays together," she quickly explained.

"Yeah," said her mom, "I think he just thought it would be fun for you guys to spend a few hours together for a change. That's all."

Lizzie bit her lip. "Well," she said slowly, "when you put it like that—"

"Oh, don't worry," said Mrs. McGuire, waving her hand. "Your dad just . . . he doesn't always understand where your *priorities* are."

"My priorities?" Lizzie echoed.

"Well, yeah, sure. I mean, your friends are the people that you *want* to spend time with. Your family are the people that you *have* to spend time with."

"But that's not how I feel exactly—" Lizzie said, trying to defend herself.

Her mother cut her off. "Honey, I get it. Your dad's just a little slower when it comes to that sort of thing." Rising off the bed, she proudly held up the boots. "Well, look at that. I think these look perfect. You can totally wear these boots tomorrow night."

Lizzie took the newly cleaned boots and stared at her mother. "Yeah," she said, but her tone was less than enthusiastic. Suddenly, she felt incredibly guilty and selfish—and worried that she'd really messed up and hurt her dad.

"Have fun," said Mrs. McGuire lightly. Then she waved and walked out.

Why do I suddenly have a heavy feeling in my stomach?... I've got to stop having these talks with Mom!

CHAPTER SIX

The next day, Matt and Lanny waddled across the McGuires' backyard, dumped arm-loads of Operation Mummy supplies onto the picnic table, and plopped down.

"What a waste," said Matt. "All the planning, all the hard work. And for what? Nothing."

Lanny nodded, then smiled.

"I guess you're right," said Matt. "We do have a reason to celebrate. I mean, it's not every day that the bully who tortures you ends up in traction." He laughed. "And you'd think he'd remember where the tire swing was!"

Matt had heard the whole story on the street. That nasty Heywood Briggs had gone skateboarding after school—on a board he'd stolen from a smaller kid. But Heywood wasn't paying attention, and as he zoomed across the playground he smacked right into a tire swing that sent him flying into the school Dumpster.

"Yeow," said Matt, envisioning the collision. "That had to hurt."

Lanny nodded in enthusiastic agreement.

Matt gestured to the mountain of plastic wrap and honey on the table in front of them. "Guess we don't need any of this stuff until his body cast comes off," he told Lanny.

But Lanny disagreed. He pounded the table with his fists.

"You're right," said Matt, snapping his fingers. "We can't lose our edge. We've got to keep practicing."

The boys rose from the table and gathered their Operation Mummy supplies.

All we need now is a practice dummy, thought Matt. And the word "dummy" makes my choice all too easy. "Oh, Lizzie!" he called as they headed inside.

Lucky for Lizzie, she wasn't home. She was already on her way to the Digital Bean, where Gordo and Miranda were in the middle of another "life coach" conversation.

"Look," Gordo complained as he lounged on one of the café's couches, "I've been the ball. I've been the pins. There's no *way* I'm gonna be the shoes. And I'm still feeling gutter ball, gutter ball, gutter ball. See, my fingers are even beginning to swell."

Leafing through a fashion magazine on a nearby chair, Miranda sighed in exasperation. She'd tried everything with Gordo: positive reinforcement, visualization, relaxation, cookies. It was finally time for the most drastic stage of all—the truth.

"Gordo, why does *not* being *the best* at something make your fingers swell?" she asked him pointedly. "You don't have to be the best at everything. You can do stuff *just* to have *fun.*"

Gordo blinked. "I guess. I never really thought of that," he admitted.

"No kidding," said Miranda, rolling her eyes.

"Hey, guys," said Lizzie, collapsing heavily into an overstuffed chair.

"What's up?" asked Gordo.

"Pretzel stomach," she said with a sigh. "This whole thing with my dad. It's so complicated."

"I thought you said he was cool with everything," said Gordo.

"Yeah, what happened?" asked Miranda.

"I'm not quite sure," said Lizzie slowly. "But after talking to my mom, I feel like I made the wrong decision."

"Yeah. Moms will do that to you," said Miranda.

"What would the *right* decision be?" asked Gordo.

Enough, enough! I can't handle all these questions!

"I don't know. I'm so confused," said Lizzie, leaning her head on the back of the chair and shutting her eyes.

When she opened them again, she saw

something to make her even *more* confused. Ethan Craft's hottie face was staring right down at her. He gave her one of his totally heart-stopping smiles.

"Hey, Lizzie," he said smoothly, "check you at bowling, right?"

Lizzie gulped. How could she say no to that face? "Yeah. I'll be there," she told him with certainty—until he walked away. Then she thought of her dad, sitting at home all sad, and her spirits sank again. "I think," she muttered.

CHAPTER SEVEN

Later that evening, Lizzie was jumping up and down at the Rock 'n' Bowl—because her very first turn bowling the ball had earned her a perfect strike!

"Lizzie, that was amazing!" squealed Miranda.

"Thank you, thank you!" cried Lizzie.

"Wow," said Gordo. He was truly impressed. And he wasn't the only one. Ethan Craft had been watching from the next lane. With a cool smile, he strolled over to her.

"Yo, Lizzie," he said. "You rock."

That's funny, you rock, too. We are so perfect for each other!

Lizzie had to bite her cheek to keep from doing a seriously not-cool thing—like screaming with joy right into Ethan's face. Instead she gave him a totally-down-with-it little smile and simply said, "Thanks." Then she turned and did her very best to walk back to the end of the lane without falling on her face.

When Lizzie took a seat behind the scoring table, Miranda and Gordo both stood up. The life coach and her pupil walked together to the ball return.

"Bowling is good. Bowling is fun. Bowling will not make my fingers swell," Gordo chanted.

Miranda patted his shoulder. "Here," she said, handing him a cookie.

"Thank you," he mumbled between nervous bites.

Gordo picked up his ball, took his place at the end of the lane, and struck his best bowling pose. After a deep, relaxing breath, he threw the ball and watched it roll and roll and roll down the alley. Just before it reached the pins, the ball veered off and dropped into the gutter with an embarrassing *thud*. Gordo hadn't knocked over one single pin.

"Gutter ball!" he shouted with joy.

"Yeah!" cried Miranda, rushing up to him.

"That was horrible!" he exclaimed with a grin.

"The worst I've ever seen!" she agreed.

"Oh, thank you, Miranda," said Gordo sincerely. "I couldn't stink this bad without you."

"So, uh, how are your fingers?" she asked.

Gordo held them up. "There are no signs of swelling," he declared proudly. It looked like he had finally learned to do something just for the fun of it!

Ethan called over to Gordo from his own lane. "Yo, Gor-don! I thought you said you were good at this."

"He is!" replied Miranda.

"Yeah. I'm a *great* bowler!" agreed Gordo.

Ethan looked more confused than usual. He frowned at them. "Dude," he said gravely, "you stink."

"He *worse* than stinks," said Miranda, "which is why I'm so totally proud of him."

Gordo smiled at Miranda, then he stepped over to the next lane and put his hand on

Ethan's shoulder. "Ethan," he said, "life is a journey."

Ethan frowned. In his confused mind, all this stuff about journeys was way premature. "Yeah, okay," he told Gordo. "But my ride's coming later."

Miranda sat down next to Lizzie at the scoring table. "Hey," she said.

"Oh!" said Lizzie with a huge grin. "Can you believe how much fun this is?"

"I know," she whispered. "I can't believe we're actually here with Ethan Craft!"

They quietly squealed.

"And it all worked out," Lizzie noted. "I mean, it was so simple that at first I couldn't even see it."

"What do you mean?" asked Miranda.

"I looked at tonight as a win-or-lose situation," Lizzie explained. "You know, I just needed a little perspective."

"What kind of perspective?" asked Miranda.

"Kind of like what you're going through with Gordo," said Lizzie. "Except I just put myself in my dad's shoes."

Just then, her father returned to their lane from the snack bar. "Here you go, kids," he said, setting a big tray of yummy junk food down on the scoring table. "Hot dogs, fries, and a whole lot of ketchup."

Okay, so maybe this isn't the fanciest restaurant in the world. But as long as you like the people you're with, ketchup on a plate's really not that bad.

"Looks like I'm up," said Mr. McGuire, slipping into his bowling shoes. "Watch how it's done."

"Remember, Dad," Lizzie warned him, "I'm the one with the perfect strike."

"Remember, Lizzie," he warned her, "it runs in the family."

Lizzie smiled, then she bit her lip. This was turning out to be the best night ever . . . but one thing still bothered her. "Dad," she said.

"Yeah?" he asked.

"I'm really glad you're here," Lizzie told him. "And I'm really sorry for the way that I acted."

"Hey, Lizzie," said Mr. McGuire, "I'm really glad you included me in your plans tonight. I know I'm not the coolest dad in the world, but I just miss hanging out together, that's all."

Lizzie nodded. "I guess sometimes I get caught up in my own world," she admitted. "But I've had a lot of fun. And we should do this more often."

"Hey, anytime, anywhere. I'm there," said Mr. McGuire with a smile.

"Cool," said Lizzie, watching her father pull his custom-made ball out of his personal bowling bag. "Just one more question," she added.

"Shoot," he said.

"Did you really have to bring this along?" she complained, pointing to her dad's red-white-and-blue ball with his name engraved beside the finger holes. "I mean, people are watching, Dad."

Mr. McGuire just shook his head and held up the bowling bag with his nickname engraved on it. "Sweetheart," he said, "they don't call me 'Striking Sam' because of my good looks . . . though it helps."

Lizzie looked up to find Ethan smiling at her from his lane. Lizzie smiled back. And Mr. McGuire noticed.

"Lizzie," he whispered with a raised eyebrow, "I don't think it's *me* he's watching."

"Da-a-a-d," wailed Lizzie, embarrassed.

"Hey, I can keep it *low*. I mean, *real*," he quickly corrected. "I can keep it real."

"Dad, Dad," said Lizzie cringing. "Just, bowl. *Bowl*!"

"Okay, okay," said Mr. McGuire. Then he did bowl—an amazingly perfect strike!

Lizzie, Miranda, and Gordo whooped, Ethan threw over a thumbs-up, and Mr. McGuire grinned. Then father and daughter shared a high five.

Wow, thought Lizzie, I guess my dad was right all along. Strikes *do* run in the family!

Don't close the book on Lizzie yet!
Here's a sneak peek at the next
Lizzie McGuire story. . . .

HiGH-FiVE

Adapted by Alice Alfonsi

Based on the television series, "Lizzie McGuire", created by Terri Minsky

Based on the episode written by Nancy Neufeld Callaway

Why is my life so *lame*? Lizzie McGuire asked herself one Monday morning. Lately, everything she did seemed neither seriously good nor seriously bad. Just seriously average.

As she trudged through the halls of Hillridge Junior High, Lizzie noticed some students gathering around a bulletin board. Her English teacher had just posted the grades from last Friday's big test.

Hey, she thought, quickening her pace toward the group of kids, maybe this is the day I break out of my boring rut. Maybe this is the day I finally excel at something.

"Yes! I aced it again!" cried Ricky Mercado.

Of course, he aced it, thought Lizzie. Ricky was reading Shakespeare back when I was still sounding out the vowels in *See Spot Run*.

Standing next to Ricky, Tanya Washington gave him a high five. "Look out, Harvard!" she squealed. Tanya, who had also made an A, was the regional spelling bee champ. When Lizzie was under pressure, Lizzie was lucky if she could even spell *bee*.

After Ricky and Tanya strode away, Lizzie moved closer to the bright orange roster her English teacher had posted. Students' names were listed alphabetically.

Lippin, Mattson, McGuire, Lizzie read silently to herself. Then her eyes moved to see the grade beside her name.

Surprise. Another B. It's not bad, it's just a B. Boring. Bland. Blah . . . Blah *again.*

Lizzie sighed and continued her walk down the hall. It was *not* a happy walk. Every ten feet she walked past some amazingly accomplished classmate.

First there was Ivana Peters, bending and stretching by her locker. As a small child,

Ivana had studied ballet in Moscow. Now she was performing professionally in her spare time, and everyone expected her two talented feet to take her to the top of the toe-dancing world.

After Ivana, Lizzie walked past a group of science geeks. They were all gathered around Larry Tudgeman because he'd won yet another science fair prize over the weekend. His winning entry was some sort of way complicated study of a molecule.

Ever notice that *everyone* seems to be great at something?

Tudgeman's science fair groupies will win Nobel prizes someday, thought Lizzie. And what am I destined to win? The Always Average award? How lame is that?

Lizzie shook her head. This whole super-achiever thing was really starting to bug her. Just then, Lizzie spotted her two best friends, Miranda Sanchez and David "Gordo" Gordon.

Panic attack averted, she thought, striding over to them. After all, being totally average and boring isn't so bad when your friends are right there beside you!

Unfortunately, Lizzie quickly had to admit that her best friends were far from average and boring. As Lizzie walked over to them, Miranda was holding up this piece of chunky silver jewelry for Gordo to see.

"Hey, great necklace," Lizzie told Miranda. It was totally cool and unique.

"Thanks," said Miranda with a grin. "I made it out of a soda can."

Lizzie furrowed her brow.

**See what I mean?
All I can do with a soda can
is recycle it.**

"No, no," Gordo told Miranda, "don't turn that way—I'm losing my shot."

Lizzie grimaced when she noticed the digital camera in Gordo's hands. He was filming Miranda in another one of his "typical day at Hillridge" shoots.

**Gordo's in search of his next
documentary and I can barely
take a Polaroid.**

Miranda noticed Lizzie frowning. "What's up?" she asked.

"English test grades are up," Lizzie replied.

"Another B?" guessed Miranda.

"What else?" Lizzie said. "I'm so sick of getting Bs. I want an A at something."

"Hey, you could be an actress," Gordo suggested brightly from behind his digital lens. "You look pretty good through the camera."

"You think?" asked Lizzie hopefully.

Gordo nodded supportively. "Sure."

"Cool," said Lizzie. She did a little spin in place, trying to make her hair whip around like Jessica Simpson.

Wow, thought Lizzie. Me. An actress—

Unfortunately, Lizzie failed to notice Gordo's backpack sitting on the floor two feet away. As she tripped over it and went flying, Gordo frowned. He moved the camera away from his eye and blinked at Lizzie.

"Or a stuntwoman," he amended.

From the floor, Lizzie groaned, now totally convinced she would *never* be good at anything.

Sorry! That's the end of the sneak peek for now. But don't go nuclear! To read the rest, all you have to do is look for the next title in the Lizzie McGuire series—